# The First of the Undying
## *A Zompire Tale*

**Written by Lane West**

*Cover Art & Inspiration by Jo Swigart*

The First of the Undying

Copyright © 2025 Lane West

Artist Copyright © 2025 Jo Swigart



This is a work of fiction and original artwork. Similarities to real people, places or events are entirely coincidental.

Lane West

*To my best friend Jo for always inspiring me through her art and actions. And to my husband thank you for your love, your patience, and for always believing in me.*

# Contents

# Part 1

# Chapter 1

He hadn't been a vampire for very long.

He clutched his prey tightly, the thought lingering. His teeth held their death grip where her neck met her shoulder, and he could sense that her death was near. There was really no need to hold her so close that he could feel her warmth slipping away, but he needed her. There was something almost human left inside him that longed to wrap his arms around a female and hold her close. He longed for the warm bodily embrace of a lover, a friendly hug from a sister, the safe assurance from a mother. His natural instincts, the predator, always took over and all he could do was let his mind wander while he fed. Just for a moment, she had pierced that dark chasm of loneliness gnawing at him from within, and he was caught between the need to feed and the aching desire for connection.

"I'm still new to this" he thought aloud.

Her limp body collapsed to the ground as he sighed and turned his back, walking away with a predatory grace. He needed to feed like any beast, to survive. He preferred the mundane meals of a human diet or stalking the woods for deer. It was only this year that he had the need to prey on mankind. As he hunted the city for his human prey, he learned that he preferred young women. Their essence was intoxicating and always kept the promise of a sweet, herbal feast. The men he had slaughtered were heavy with musk and spices. A harsh flavor that he found unappealing. They always resisted, or at least tried to resist him, and he didn't care for the disorder of a messy kill.

Am I still new to this?

He was consumed with the notion that even though it had been two decades he was still considered 'new'. His vampiric body aged much slower than his human body ever did. Darious, his mentor, had explained that one vampire year equated to twenty human years. By that account, he was barely one. Yet, in his brief one year as a vampire, he learned to live among the humans. Not just walking or passing through their world, truly living there with them. Feeding on this prey was not at all common. Darious had cautioned him about numerous dangers he now faced as a fledgling vampire. Despite the wild stories, it was the Reaving that terrified him the most. That is where he found himself now, and he despised it more than any other any other legend.

The Wolf Moon in January, was just a few months away. At the end of their twentieth year, vampires were the most ravenous that they ever would be. Not at their creation, not at their ending. Only twenty years in and it lasted up to the Wolf Moon. Their entire being and all their senses pushed them to feast almost non-stop. Only human blood provided the necessary calories and fat to satisfy them throughout the Reaving and ready them for what lay ahead. During this period, he didn't even crave his favorite meal of fried alligator and potatoes.

The Reaving would conclude, and he would need to hibernate like a bear during the frost of winter. His vampiric body would enter such a profound slumber he wouldn't fully awaken for nearly a decade. His nightly feedings had to be almost perfectly timed now to keep up with the transformations that were overtaking him. Vampires always underwent metamorphosis during their rest and many emerged with physical changes. The predatory state they assumed during the hunt evolved into a more powerful and intimidating beast. Their brain waves also shifted, often granting them new magickal abilities that they needed to learn. All of this demanded a significant amount of human blood to maintain cellular balance.

When he was just a few days old, he was surprised to discover that vampires didn't require human blood for survival, at least not immediately. He maintained his human diet and only drank blood while hunting with Darious during their full moon rituals. He was born and raised around Assumption Parish in Louisiana and had always heard tales of vampires. Braum Stoker's Dracula had left its imprint on the world of people's imagination, and he expected to burn up in the sunlight or sleep in a coffin. However, these were all fictional stories, loosely inspired by the real histories.

"A vampire doesn't require human blood until they hit the twenty-year mark. That final year is known as the Reaving because nothing but human blood will do. Initially, you'll need it once a month, but during the last three months, you'll have to feed every day."

Darious' words replayed in his mind as he walked past the familiar streetlamps on his way home. For the last ten years, he had been alone while Darious traveled. Reuniting with his mentor had helped dispel the encroaching shadows within him. Darious' enormous grin always drew his attention and warmed his heart. Standing nearly 6'3" with a bodybuilder's physique, Darious had a striking dark complexion that made his bright smile shine even more.

Colin was deep in thought about his new life when he made his last turn home. The broad avenues of the Garden District in New Orleans were always welcoming. As he drew nearer, it felt as though his house came to life, rising up and becoming more grand and imposing, almost as if it were alive. It would stretch to the skies upon seeing him. The house was painted in cream with dark cream trim, complemented by black shutters and a black iron fence. The scalloped edging on the rooftop matched the decorative balcony on the second floor. Colin had been drawn to its asymmetrical Italianate style when Darious suggested he settle in this city.

With just a few more steps, Colin caught the scent of Darious amidst the evening fog. The aroma was so potent that Colin could nearly taste it, a mix of bitter manglier and sweet honey. Darious's fragrance seamlessly intertwined with the jasmine and honeysuckle that adorned the district's streets. Many homes here featured stunning gardens and towering trees in their late bloom, the entire neighborhood enveloped in the season's final, fragrant breath.

The air was thick with misty humidity, muffling the lively noises of the city behind. As Colin approached his front gate, a sharp scent of decay hit him, catching in his throat.

Humans. Long-dead humans…and Darious. Before he could process this, Colin found himself in his foyer, surveying the scene. Darious was cautiously backing into the parlor to the right, with three long-dead humans standing before him. Colin couldn't believe what he was seeing.

"What the fuck, Darious!" Colin's predatory instincts kicked in aggressively as he snarled the words. His vampire mouth stretched wide, almost reaching his ears, and every tooth elongated to a sharp, spear-like point. His deep blue eyes darkened to a deep grey as he glared at Darious again.

"What the fuck, Darious! What *are* they?"

"Now, don't you fucking move Colin!" Darious's Cajun accent slipped through when he was under pressure, revealing his background despite years of trying to suppress it.

Colin's dark eyes darted over the trio in front of him. These three lifeless figures were fixated on his mentor. They wore regular street attire, but one unmistakably appeared to have been a tourist. His khaki trousers were paired with a bright blue fanny pack that had long since sagged from his waist. A clear green visor hung ominously, partially covering his droopy right eye. Their skin seemed barely attached to life, clinging tightly to exposed bones or sagging where muscles used to be.

Colin stifled a gasp as the overpowering odor of the corpses assaulted him again. He nearly vomited when all three of them suddenly jerked their heads back with a gruesome crack. Their jaws fell to their chests, unleashing a piercing, immobilizing scream that was both sharp and deafening.

Growling. Colin didn't realize he was doubled over in agony, clutching his ears and growling. He kept shouting "what the fuck" at Darious. The eerie tune of the corpse song had rattled his nerves so intensely that he was compelled to retreat, unable to resist. Once their shrill echoes ceased, the only sound that reached Colin was the deep voice of his mentor, now somewhere close to him.

"Zombis. Colin, they're zombis," he said, offering his hand to help Colin stand up.

"Zombies," Colin muttered under his breath, struggling to comprehend the concept.

"Zombis."

"Zombies or Zombis, what's the fucking difference? Dead is dead, and it shouldn't be wandering around screaming in my house!" Colin snapped.

Darious hurriedly grabbed a small black pouch from the parlor. He swiftly slipped it into the zombi man's fanny pack before guiding Colin out of the entryway. The three zombis grunted and groaned as they shuffled through the front door, vanishing into the night as if some invisible magick had spirited them away. Colin realized that their foul odor was already dissipating with them.

In the parlor, the two settled down beside a large fireplace. Colin was still processing the recent events when Darious passed him a glass of whiskey. Colin accepted it with thanks, careful to avoid spilling it on his shirt as Darious began to speak.

"Drink, it will help with the senses…and the predator."

After a quick drink, Colin realized the lingering scent of a long-dead human had disappeared. This calmed him, allowing his vampiric features to revert to their usual, handsome appearance. He exchanged a questioning look with Darious, and they settled more comfortably into two red chairs by the fire.

"The zombis originate from a High Priest here in New Orleans. He is an authentic Voodoo practitioner, and his ancestors trace their roots back to Haiti. They possess power, spells, poisons, and formulas for both creation and destruction of zombis."

"Why have you never told me about them?" …because I'm still new to this. Colin thought silently, answering his own question. Running his fingers through his dark brown hair, he took another sip of whiskey, feeling his face and vampiric muscles relax further. He had learned early on that a vampire's entire body transformed when they were in hunting mode, a fact he observed while deer hunting with Darious under the full moon.

"Look here," his mentor instructed. Colin peered into the water's reflections, observing his transformed physique and noting how his muscles had become perfectly defined and prominent. As a human, he had always been in good shape—standing 6 feet tall, lean, and straight with almost black hair, cut short but longer on top, always framing his deep blue eyes. The vampiric transformation had added an extra 30 pounds of muscle, causing his clothes to become uncomfortably tight.

When he was hunting or under extreme stress, his vampire features would emerge, shifting him into a monstrous form. His arms became exceptionally strong and elongated, while his spine stretched, increasing his height and making him more intimidating. However, it was his mouth that always startled him the most, a gaping maw filled with razor-sharp teeth that seemed to split his head in two. His powerful jaws extended to accommodate this fearsome set of teeth, ensuring that any prey he chased stood no chance of escaping.

"Did you hear me?" Darious snapped. "One of these days Colin you're going to get stuck in that knucklehead of yours!"

"Yea, zombis and a damn angry High Priest." Colin smirked.

Darious grinned a long while as they both were pleased to be away from the zombis. They took a moment to pour more whiskey before Colin began again.

"What were they doing here and what do they want?"

"Well, I owe their master. You see the zombis serve the High Priest until he deems their debt paid. That's when he rests them in the grave, and they are finally at peace. But it was him, the High Priest, that helped me escape the bayou slave trade back when I was still a human." Darious' face fell a bit as the memories of his enslavement lingered.

"He brought me to our beloved Vampire Queen, and she gave me the strength to avenge my fallen family and break free of chains."

Colin paused cold. Queen. The word swirled around in his head as he stared patiently into the fire. He didn't even know there was such a thing. More evidence that he was for sure new to this.

# Part 2

# Chapter 2

The Wolf Moon was only a week away now. Colin had been feeling her pull for the past month as his body and mind were wracked with all the information he had received from Darious. It had been months since the zombis, and Colin had not seen them again. Nor could he forget them or what Darious had divulged. He had been a vampire for twenty years and not one word about zombis, priests or vampire queens. He couldn't help but wonder why Darious had held back, but as the moon crept in on him Colin started to understand.

The Reaving took full control of him now. There was no human that could get near him without his body flashing into the predator. The attack was always imminent, and all his senses were hijacked by the need to feed. Darious had taken him out into the country to one of those old cotton farms where slavery had been prominent. Colin knew that Darious had lived a rough human life, but imagining that hulking, powerful figure as anything but strong was nearly impossible. Here and now, however, slavery is long gone, and nothing was around but wildlife, large open forest lands and running water somewhere close by. It was beautiful and Colin was grateful for the peace it instilled in him.

His thoughts were deep, and it took a great deal of effort now for him to break out of them. Darious often snapped or clapped his hands to grab Colin back out of his mind. His thoughts were no longer alone, not anymore. What was once a beckoning darkness that threatened to swallow him whole had become thoughts of her. She had a mental connection with him that began with the Winter Solstice, and she filled him completely. The Vampire Queen, Aradia, was always in his mind and she took pleasure in poking around in his head. Despite this she was also incredibly divulging, which was not something Colin expected when Darious had revealed her existence.

Aradia, as far as Colin was allowed to know, was once one of five vampire queens. They each had their own covens and were allowed to create vampires at will. Each of them chose humans who had the potential to increase their power or serve their needs in other ways. Darious was chosen because he had a rare ability as a vampire, he was approachable and easy for new vampires to be around. His skills as a mentor were not limited to a few, but he was there for all Aradia's chosen since his rebirth. All the way through the Reaving he had been with her coven and helped guide and raise them. Aradia's coven consisted entirely of males. She had never selected a female to join because it had caused problems before. This issue was not unique to her; all the queens faced challenges when dealing with female vampires.

Colin knew now that there were only three queens left, and all the vampires alive today were male. He did not yet know what had happened - just that it was long ago. As he wandered the vast porch of the cotton mansion, he could feel winter's chill starting to release its grip. He stood with his arms and face in this sun, soaking in the rays as Aradia began a check of his physical state. He could feel her mind and magick all over inside of him. He found it comforting that she was so gentle, and it also made him feel like he was connected to someone in ways that he had never been before. Her motherly touch was something Colin had never experienced. And despite her immense and terrible power she calmed him, and he felt secure in their bond.

"She's our mother, you know."

Colin had been so preoccupied he did not hear Darious approach. He extended a massive paw, grabbing Colin's shoulder and helping him to a chair on the porch.

"She is always with me now. Will it stay this way forever?"

"Yes and no. Like any mother she knows when she is not needed and when she is. It isn't easy guiding a whole coven and keeping them on the path you know." Darious said as he handed Colin a glass of human blood.

"It's fresh, drink up. You're going to need all that for your sleep."

Colin hesitated to grab the glass, he was tired and didn't really want to feed right now. But Aradia gently pushed him and in a single gulp the glass was empty. He smiled feeling deeply satisfied as Darious sat next to him and his stories began again.

"You'll be laid to rest in the queen's crypt. She built it for us long ago and all her young rest there while they go through the change, after the Reaving leaves them. It's where we are most connected to her and all her efforts will go into helping your metamorphosis, growing your mind and body. She will also keep your mind in hibernation mode, so the predator doesn't explode out and wake you up. We are never more vulnerable or more protected than when we are in our sleep with her. I'll be keeping tabs on you too."

Colin looked down and let Darious's words soak into him. Ten years of rest and Aradia is with you the entire time. He frowned a bit.

"Is that not dangerous for Aradia? I know she is all powerful, but does that not put her in a vulnerable state to be tending to me and however many others in the crypts?"

Colin watched his mentor mull this thought over while sipping on a glass of whiskey. His head gently nodded as though he were listening to someone else, and Colin knew it had to be their queen.

"It is very dangerous, and not an easy task. That's why she never creates more than three children in one go. They are always well timed too so that each sleeps together. Same location, same timing, same everything. Aradia also sleeps with them putting her body into a deep slumber so she can focus all her efforts on the task of helping you change. But make no mistake – she is not vulnerable. An army of her children stands between her and anyone who would wish her newborns harm. They were all raised for just this task, and they are much older and more powerful than I am."

Colin stayed on the porch a bit longer, absorbing the advice from his mentor. Darious elaborated on manners, expectations, and what felt like every essential piece of knowledge. Once Darious finished, Colin closed his eyes for a brief rest. His thoughts drifted over the stories he'd just heard, trying to absorb it all. He stretched his legs to lengthen his spine and took a deep breath. Suddenly, the smell of death wafted in, jolting him to sit up, alert and tense.

Dead humans, zombis had just appeared at the edge of the porch. Colin was surprised they could reach this far or be so distant from their master. As he quickly surveyed the group, he recognized three of them. They were the same trio that had nearly deafened him months ago back home. However, this time they weren't alone. At least nine corpses stood before them, all shuffling and huddling together in a line.

*I fucking hate the zombis*, he thought.

*"They are not to be trusted, Colin. Don't let them near you."*

Aradia's voice quietly infiltrated Colin's thoughts, and he remained motionless. Her voice was calming and richer than he had anticipated. He wished to hear more, yet she remained silent. It was the first time she had spoken to him in such a manner, and he found himself yearning for more interactions with her. However, the increasing odor of decaying humans jolted his focus back to the zombis.

Darious was quick to retrieve a small black pouch from his pocket and work his way down the stairs to the zombis. All of their eyes were on him as he dropped the pouch in the tourist zombi's fanny pack, and zipped it shut. This time, the fanny pack slipped off the fading waist of the corpse and as it hit the ground all the zombis started to panic. They shoved into each other flailing their dead arms about, smacking each other one by one until they all appeared to smack the tourist zombi. Each of their movements elicited a wretched grunt and soon they were in a circle around the dead tourist, and Darious.

Colin watched the unfolding events half amused and half worried. He wasn't sure how long Darious had been dealing with the dead, but it was clearly long enough that he was not at all bothered by their endless shuffling, or their stench. Darious retrieved the fanny pack from the ground, unbuckling it from the dead man's rotted body. As he slung it over one shoulder and under the opposite arm, he quickly tightened the strap and buckled it in place. It looked a bit like a sad attempt at a messenger bag to Colin. Having it secured to the tourist zombi once more seemed to make them all happy.

Colin was sure that there had to be some ounce of humanity left in them to elicit such a show of relief. His mind started to mull this over when he felt a sharp nudge from Aradia. Colin pushed the thought away, looking back at the scene. One of the zombis was staring him down.

She was not rotten like the others, though he could still smell death deep inside her bones. Somewhere around 5'8" she reached just under Darious' shoulders and had long blonde hair that was still intact. Her skin bore a light farmer's tan around her exposed shoulders, and it was evident that in life she had been wearing blue jeans and a tank top that accentuated her perfectly feminine shape. She had piercing brown eyes that felt inviting, and Colin was instantly curious. He didn't notice that he was standing on the grass in front of the crowd, and she began to slowly push towards him.

The more Colin gazed into her eyes, the more alive she seemed. He was mesmerized as she transformed back into her human beauty, her skin now radiant under the sunlight. Her hair revived, softly swaying in the breeze. Her lips were full, pink, and enticing, compelling him with the urge to kiss and savor them. She stood just a few steps away, and he could sense her warmth drawing closer to him.

Colin's anticipation shattered like glass when searing pain engulfed every inch of his body. He crashed to the ground, his vision blurring as the once mesmerizing beauty transformed into a ghastly, semi-rotten corpse looming over him. Her eyes burned with hatred, and fury erupted from her like a violent storm. She savagely tore into him with claws sharper than daggers, teeth as vicious as a beasts, and bones that struck like hammers.

Desperately, he reached for the predator within, but agony immobilized him, leaving his vampire body limp. His attempts to track her relentless attacks were useless, as the stench of her decomposition overwhelmed his senses, triggering a torrent of vomiting. In a frantic bid to push away the nightmare, he thrust out an arm, only to watch in horror as his skin shredded open, and blood gushed from his exposed, quivering muscles.

When Colin finally got control of his stomach, he collapsed to the ground giving into the soft grass. He managed to roll onto his back and the pain told him that she had torn through all his back muscles leaving him lying there. Her scent of death had faded for a moment before rolling back towards him. He knew that another attack was on its way and all he could do was wait for her. His heart was pounding; he could taste the adrenaline rushing through him and beating against open wounds all over his body. He sucked in what he thought was his last living breath when the sky above him cracked open with a thunderous boom.

Aradia descended from the sky with what appeared to be a small battalion of vampires. Her crimson dress reminded him of roses, its hem fluttering elegantly with her every motion. Her arms were bare, and she moved them with exaggerated gestures, dancing to a silent melody. When they touched down and surrounded him, he felt concealed by their dark, militant attire. None of them glanced in his direction, focused instead on firing their weapons. The sound of gunfire and weaponry drowned out the noises of the forest, making him wonder how any zombis could have survived.

Aradia finished her dance and soared back into the air, hovering just above Colin. Her long black hair whipped around, shielding his bloodied eyes from the waning January sun. A wave of heat surged through him as she extended her arms towards the unseen dead, and flames erupted around her. She unleashed these flames like a living flamethrower, fire streaming from her arms, body, and even her hair, forming a circle around them. She returned to the ground, straddled Colin and pressed one of his broken hands to her chest. The last thing he saw were her red and yellow eyes gazing deeply into his before he finally lost consciousness.

# Part 3

# Chapter 3

Colin winced slightly as he opened his eyes, feeling like sand was beneath his eyelids, scratching each time he blinked. In his exhaustion, he imagined a dust storm taking over his vision each time he tried to concentrate. The last thing he remembered was lying in the yard, bleeding on the grass. Now, he found himself in what appeared to be a dimly lit bedroom, right in the middle of a large, soft bed. Several candles were aglow, and a small fireplace stood without flames. A deep breath revealed the faint scent of recently extinguished embers.

He stretched both hands to the ceiling to check out the damage done by the zombi girl. He only saw bandages and wrappings. He was able to move all his fingers so that had to be a good sign.

"A good sign indeed, my son."

In person, her voice was so melodic and captivating that it took Colin by surprise. He attempted to sit up straight to greet Aradia more appropriately, but his body refused to cooperate.

"Stop fighting me. You're not yet healed, and I need to take measure of the damage he has done to you."

"He," Colin paused realizing how scratchy his throat felt.

"A woman zombi did this."

Aradia had been seated beside his bed when he noticed her moving closer. She shifted onto the bed next to his weary, beaten body. Her eyes locked onto his, and she gradually placed her hands just inches from his skin. Colin felt her magick flowing through him, examining injuries he didn't know existed.

"Make no mistake, the zombis never disobey their master. This was an attack by their High Priest. He has never been so bold before, but he has always threatened our family. Now, roll over, let me see your back."

Despite the difficulty, Colin complied. His muscles were so battered that he couldn't help but speculate about where exactly the zombi had attacked him. He used his legs to assist with the final effort to roll onto his stomach, feeling Aradia resume her examination. Her magick was more than just a comforting warmth within him; it seemed to be applying an invisible remedy that eased the worst of his pain.

The sharp, electric jolts of pain gradually softened into a dull ache. When her magick settled into his lower back and radiated down his sciatic nerve into his legs, he let out a relieved groan.

"Thank you. Tell me, how bad is it?"

"You will be scarred on your back for sure. I think your arms will be ok and your face has already started to recover. You will be your handsome self once more." She smiled at him and he felt deeply comforted by her. He noticed his mother's eyes were still red and yellow but their heat and anger were gone now. All that remained was her stillness, deep and caring.

"Zombis are for the most part harmless. They do their masters bidding to pay off some debt they owe. A lot of them don't deserve the punishment the High Priest forces upon them. They are tricked into service and those are the ones you saw like the zombi man with his silly little bag. He was clearly a traveler that did not know any better. An easy target for any beast."

"I really do not think they are harmless. You saw what she did to me. How could something dead have that much strength? Or even skill to overpower a vampire?"

"She was a blood sworn, a witch, in her lifetime. Sometimes I have even seen those deadly zombis be totally normal human women, but they have some ancient witch bloodline that is long dormant in their family. The High Priest and his kind, they know this. So, they trick them into service, or they use their magick and force them into slavery with the zombi curse."

Aradia carefully adjusted Colin's position on the bed, gently maneuvering him until he was comfortably propped up against a heap of pillows. Each movement seemed to drain him, his eyelids drooping with fatigue. She meticulously arranged the pillows around him, ensuring he could sit upright without strain. Once satisfied, she picked up a delicate stemmed glass filled with deep red wine, its aroma rich and inviting. Beside her, on a small wooden tray, sat a warm glass of blood for Colin, its surface shimmering softly in the dim light. Settling into the chair next to him, Aradia resumed her explanation, her voice steady as she spoke.

"You see my son, only a witch could have a strong enough connection to the High Priest to act in such a manner. Most zombis can scream their terrible song – which can paralyze a vampire momentarily, if they intend it. But other than that, they shuffle about. They do try biting humans here and there but it's not that often. The witch bloods are as you now know, a different story entirely. They can attack without mercy, they have incredible speed, and they can even pass along the zombi curse through biting if you're a human. And as you know they can use their witch magick too. So whatever they were gifted with as living souls they carry with them into their slave form."

Colin had finished half his glass of blood when Aradia paused for her own drink. He remembered the zombi witch and how she turned from rotten flesh into an appealing woman, and he shivered.

"She changed right in front of me. I couldn't take my eyes off her she was just instantly there, and suddenly so beautiful." He said a bit shamefully.

"I know. I saw her through your eyes and damn her. I couldn't kill her she escaped as soon as my fire spell was cast."

"Spell?" Colin cut in.

Aradia gazed at him with a gentle smile that illuminated her features. The soft, wavering glow painted her face in warm hues, highlighting her timeless beauty. Her skin, kissed by the sun, bore a subtle tan that contrasted elegantly with her sultry black hair. Though her years had added wisdom to her eyes, her face retained a youthful vibrancy that defied her age. High, regal cheekbones framed her serene expression, and her graceful presence was accentuated by the red silky nightgown she wore, peeking out from beneath a matching robe that draped effortlessly over her form. To him, she was a vision of ageless elegance, an eternal muse suspended in the dance of shadows and light.

"Yes, spell. I was born a witch. You see our bloodlines are heavy with witch ancestors and in my youth as a human I was a powerful witch. I come from a long line of them and that's what you saw. The vampire transition only heightened my magick powers, enabling me and my sister queens the ability to create new life. Before you ask, yes you too are from a witch bloodline. You felt the heat from my flames, yes?"

Colin nodded slowly, his head bobbing in silent agreement, unwilling to let even a whisper escape his lips and disturb the truth that was now being woven together before him. His eyes were fixed, absorbing every detail as if capturing the essence of a puzzle finally coming into focus.

"It wasn't just heat, my son. You were on fire with me. I merged my powers with yours to create a banishing flame which set the zombis ablaze and set a protective perimeter around the property. They no longer burn but the power of the flame is there protecting us. I cannot do this with all my children. Your blood is special and full of ancient power that we have not seen in hundreds of years."

Colin opened his mouth to pose another question, but Aradia gently placed a finger on her lips, signaling him to be quiet. "Rest now," she whispered, her voice soothing yet firm. He remained seated against a stack of pillows, thankful for the support they provided. A dull, pulsing ache started to throb around his eyes, intensifying with every heartbeat. It felt as though a vise was squeezing his temples, threatening to crush his brain stem. Colin hoped that staying upright might alleviate the mounting pressure inside his head.

Overwhelmed with fatigue, he no longer concerned himself with bloodlines or magick. He simply fell asleep.

# Chapter 4

"You slept for three whole days and nights. It's damn good to see you outside again!"

Darious approached Colin with a grin that seemed to radiate under the evening sun, his teeth gleaming like polished pearls. Colin took in his surroundings on the expansive back deck of the mansion. The gentle rustle of leaves in the breeze and the distant chirping of birds reached his ears, but he barely registered them. The last thing he remembered was collapsing into his bed, his temples throbbing with a relentless headache. Now, he found himself reclined in a plush lounge chair, his legs stretched out comfortably onto a small white ottoman, the warm wood beneath him grounding him in the present moment.

"Damn good to see you." Colin grinned. He started to look around the property to get a better idea of where he was, but his eyes were stung by evening light.

"We thought some fresh air would be good. For you and for us! We got the maids upstairs cleaning your room now."

Colin couldn't help but chuckle at Darious' playful teasing. His laughter was interrupted by a sharp twinge that had him pressing gingerly against his left ribs. His eyes drifted downward, taking in the sight of his own body. He wore a snug white tank top, the fabric clinging to his torso, and a pair of matching sweatpants that hugged his calves, the attire crisp and clean against his olive skin. His gaze lingered on his right arm, now a canvas of scars from the zombi attack.

The memory of the creature tearing into his forearms flashed in his mind, and he had half-expected to see his arms still swathed in bandages or rendered useless. Instead, his skin bore testament to the ordeal, with jagged, claw-like scars stretching from wrist to elbow. Each scar told its own story, the jagged lines crisscrossing in at least five different directions. A grim map of the zombi's relentless assault.

"I should have warned you. It just wasn't the time but I'm sorry."

"No, don't do that. It's not your fault Darious." Colin tried to soothe his mentor. He hated the regret that was taking over Darious' face.

"You were standing in the middle of them. How did you get away?"

"When the zombi girl started to move towards you I tried to push the group away to get to you. I was yelling your name, but they all grabbed a hold of me and started their damn song. They focused its energy on me." Darious shuddered with the memory.

"It was only about a minute but by that time she had already struck you at least ten times. She just went off like a jaguar. I've never seen anything like it. After their damned song stopped, I was able to push through them and tried to grab her, but she kept on attacking you. I managed to grab one of her hands as she went for your throat and then Aradia showed up and she slipped off. She broke her hand off her body to get away. Like a coyote caught in a trap."

Colin was absorbed in the story trying to picture it. Two powerful vampires overwhelmed by zombis. He was still new to this.

# Part 4

# Chapter 5

Sam had been a member of Aradia's coven since before the Vikings invaded England. As a human he lived in a small mountain village next to the Norwegian sea. His entire lineage had always been warriors and this is what drew Aradia to him. He was well over 6 feet tall, and his medium length blonde hair was pulled back in a knot. His full beard was well trimmed, and his piercing blue eyes were scanning the forest borders.

Since the High Priest's attack Sam and his coven mates had been on full alert. They took turns patrolling the perimeter to ensure that Aradia's magickal barrier did not get breached. With his vampire ears he could make out Darious and Colin behind him on the deck. They were both talking and it gave him hope that his new brother was going to be okay. It's not often that zombis attack but Sam had been alive long enough to know that it does happen.

Sam was making his final round of this area when he smelled something new in the air. It wasn't vampiric, swamp creatures, deer or any of the usual suspects. It wasn't dead either – it was human, but different.

"Zac, there's something here on the south perimeter." Sam said aloud so his brothers in arms could hear. His earpiece was always turned on and listening, though being vampires, they didn't really need them.

A black and red fog began to creep towards him from the tree line just off to his right. It moved like a massive python in a river. It shifted right and left winding its way over the green lawn.

"Zac, Jarrod – I think we have a breach."

Sam was talking to his brothers in arms and taking several slow and steady steps back towards the mansion. He didn't dare turn around and leave his back exposed to whatever this fog was. It kept moving closer to him and soon it encircled him reminding him of Ouroboros eating his own tail.

"Brothers!" he yelled with all his might. But Sam didn't hear them anymore, he couldn't sense the mansion, the trees, or even the wildlife. Only this fog that was now surrounding him and rising to go beyond his height.

The mysterious red and black fog faded, and the smell of long dead flesh took over the smells of the outdoors. Sam soon found himself surrounded by an entire group of zombis whose bodies appeared from fog and quickly took solid forms. As he turned and aimed his M-4 at each of their faces they would grin and grunt. Some even groaned as though the physical manifestation process was somehow painful.

It didn't take long for Sam to catch a glimpse of her. A female zombi with what was once blonde hair. He noticed her missing right hand and she grimaced as though she could read his mind.

"Brothers, I'm in trouble!!" Sam yelled as he unleashed all the power of the weapon in his hand. He spun from one direction to another firing as many bullets as he could into the heads of the zombis that were encircled around him. They fell one after the other and until only she remained, and half her face exploded when his last bullet squarely lodged into her cheek bone.

When she fell to the ground in a sloppy pile Sam saw that her final act against him was to raise her left hand to the sky. She stretched her boney hand straight up and her rotten skin fell away revealing the depth of the decay. A guttural scream pushed forth from what remained of her lungs and Sam collapsed into a ball on the ground, all of his nerves on fire and causing his muscles to jerk and spasm uncontrollably.

Her last song lasted about thirty seconds and Sam's relief from her grip was instantly halted by a new and strange smell. Earthen herbs, musk, spices and magick. Powerful and old, ancient and metallic like decades of death and pain. Sam forced himself upright and realized his gun was no longer in his hands. He snapped his head left, then right searching for this new danger that was now somewhere near him. His eyes passed over the zombis and they were all unmoving. Some were blown backwards by the power of his gun hitting their heads. They fell either in piles or just onto their backs – none were moving, and none were the source of this new smell.

"You won't find me in them anymore. Damaged goods."

The voice was male and held a thick Cajun accent. He was clearly from this area, but Sam could not see him anywhere. He kept turning in circles until he appeared about ten feet away, his back towards the woods.

"I believe you're looking for me." The man smiled, white teeth sneering back at Sam.

"Well, take a good gander."

He was about six inches shorter than Sam, he guessed maybe the man was 5'8" or 5'9". Medium black skin and wearing a white cotton t-shirt. His muscles showed clearly through this shirt and Sam could tell he kept himself active despite his ancient presence. His hair was shaved on both sides of his head but what was on top reminded Sam of old Viking hairstyles. Only different – small braids mixed in with large braids fell neatly down to the mans straight cut jeans. A variety of jewels and relics dangled from these braids and were also fashioned around the man's wrists, neck and waist. His face looked to be around thirty, but everything about him told Sam he was much older.

"What do you want." Sam demanded.

"You. I'm here for you." The man said, walking slowly around Sam like a cat playing with its prey.

Sam reached for Aradia with his mental connection and could not feel her. He started looking for exits and could not find one as the red and black fog had returned, blocking his every out.

"I am, what your mother calls – the High Priest. But soon, you will know me as master. Shall we begin?"

Sam's heart sank hearing those words. He could smell the High Priests power rising and growing stronger. Like a tornado it circled around them both and Sam could only think that he had to fight. He would not die without going out like a warrior, and soon his predator burst forth. His whole body shifted into his full vampire, and he ripped away his black shirt to expand his chest, back, arms and spine. His eyes turned black, and his head morphed to support the now large mouth that split open to both ears. All of his vampire teeth grew to their full spear like length and his hands grew to support his massive, clawed fingers. He roared with all his might like a brown bear of his homelands, and he lunged forward towards the High Priest.

"YES!" The High Priest yelled back at him, admiring Sam's monstrous form.

As Sam launched forward the High Priest side jumped him, thrusting a handful of powder at Sam's gapping mouth. At first Sam didn't realize what had happened and jumped for the man again, this time almost reaching his left thigh with a powerful hand. But when Sam stood upright and found the man standing before him once more, his vision started to blur. His mouth was burning in pain and the taste of blood and death, and poison, started to overtake him.

"YES! You see, I cannot take a vampire except for when it's in its full vampiric form. Only then will the toxin take over and now – you are mine!" the High Priest said taking three steps back from Sam.

The High Priest began chanting a spell and dancing around tossing various herbs to the grass. Sam felt his whole body began to wither as his internal predator fell dead inside of him. His once handsome and strong face felt cold and his skin on the left side of him turned grey and stretched unnaturally tight around his now showing bones. Ice burned through his veins like shards of glass, and he screamed in terror and pain at each nerve ending that died off.

Sam kept screaming even after the ice stopped but all he could hear was a deep growling coming from his mouth. He lifted his right arm, and it was human looking, all his vampiric muscles returned to the normal human size. He lifted his left arm, and an almost skeleton arm raised in its place. The skin was tighter than it should be and there were barely any muscles remaining. This hand had long, boney fingers with claws that had looked broken down until only shards remained. There was no color other than grey and when he clenched his fist digging his claws into his palm, he heard the High Priest once more.

"Tsk, tsk. No need to violate my beautiful creation. Now you come with me."

The red and black fog that had been spinning like a tornado around them during their battle drew in closer. Sam felt the pain of loss as he watched his brothers, his mother, his family trying to get to them and never making it.

# Chapter 6

"The Wolf Moon rises tonight, and we must be in the crypts."

Aradia stood before her children, her voice steady but laced with a deep sadness as she issued her instructions. The memory of the High Priest's attack haunted them, a brutal ambush that had left them reeling with helplessness. Two nights had passed, yet the sting of their failure to rescue Sam lingered. His final, desperate plea echoed in their minds: a cry for help that had come too late. Even as they transformed into their full vampiric forms, channeling every ounce of their collective strength, they had been powerless against the impenetrable red and black barrier that stood between them and Sam.

Darious and Colin were the first to reach the barrier, and they were immediately hurled backward with a violent force. Colin's neck twisted at a precarious angle, nearly snapping, and Aradia had to channel some of her potent magick toward him to shield him from harm. As Darious regained his footing and charged forward once more, the rest of Aradia's guard had arrived, only to be relentlessly repelled by the barrier's invisible power. It was like a fierce wind, unyielding and merciless, tossing them around like leaves in a storm. Despite her relentless efforts, Aradia found herself unable to break through to reach Sam. Her only connection was through her witch's sight, a window into the nightmare unfolding at the hands of the High Priest. The sights she witnessed filled her with horror and a burning fury.

Aradia stood frozen, transfixed on Sam as he battled fiercely against the inevitable, his every move a testament to his strength, yet ultimately futile. She witnessed the High Priest approach with a sinister grin, his fingers dripping with powered poison. With deliberate malice, he threw the powder in Sam's mouth, and Aradia's heart ached as she watched the transformation begin.

Sam's once proud and muscular form, a testament to his power, began to contort under the curse's influence. His features twisted painfully, his skin shifting, becoming an unsettling mix of pallid and decayed on his left side. The zombi curse crept over him, claiming half of his body, leaving a stark contrast against his human right side.

His face, once strikingly handsome, underwent a grotesque metamorphosis. The left side sagged and grayed, skin pulling tight over bone, while the right remained smooth and youthful. His mouth, which could once stretch into a charming, wide grin, now parted awkwardly, only slightly revealing his viciously sharp canines that protruded menacingly, contrasting with the straight, human-like teeth that remained.

Aradia's heart sank as she realized that this deformed creature, this amalgamation of vampire and zombi, was now irrevocably bound to the High Priest. Sam, her beloved son, had been reduced to nothing more than a twisted servant, a new pawn in the High Priest's sinister plans.

Her group traveled together in a sleek procession of black cars, their polished exteriors gleaming under the soft sunlight. Each vehicle carried Aradia and her children closer to the historic St. Louis Cemetery #1 in the heart of New Orleans, where the past and present seemed to intertwine. As they arrived at their family's mausoleum, a faint, unsettling sensation flickered in the back of Aradia's mind, like a whisper from the depths of her subconscious.

They began their descent into the dark passages, expertly concealed from the world above, leading them exactly 33 feet beneath the surface. Once they reached the crypts, an expansive, hidden complex was unveiled, stretching beneath the bustling city like a secret labyrinth.

The air was cool and still, illuminated by strategically placed lights that cast long shadows along the stone walls.

Sam had been by her side during the planning and execution of this underground refuge. He had overseen the commissioning of skilled builders and crews who meticulously installed essential systems: the glow of electric lights, the gentle hum of power generators, the steady flow of air circulation. It was all designed to ensure their survival in this subterranean sanctuary while adhering to strict security protocols.

Moreover, Sam had taken decisive measures to safeguard their clandestine project. Each worker involved in the construction had been discreetly dismissed, ensuring that no loose ends remained. Those who had witnessed the work were either permanently silenced or bound by solemn blood oaths, swearing to protect the secret that lay beneath the city.

The sensation returned, a delicate yet persistent nudge against her consciousness, gradually seeping in as they readied Colin and her other two newborns for their lengthy slumber. Darious was guiding them through the intricate process of entering a decade-long rest, explaining the changes and events that would unfold around them during their dormant period. The nudge pressed again, more insistent this time, prompting Aradia to turn her gaze towards her bed. Its silken sheets and plush pillows invited her to join her newborns in the embrace of restfulness.

Turning her back to the crowd and the clamor, Aradia closed her eyes, inhaled deeply, and exhaled slowly. She focused her thoughts on the sensation and suddenly realized who it was, Sam. Her body went slack, and she began to collapse, but two guards caught her just in time. Her newborns and Darious watched as the guards assisted her into bed while she wept and trembled uncontrollably.

"Sam. It's Sam he is still with us!" she was overwhelmed with relief, and fear. When she finally managed to gather herself, she directed her will to her children.

"Zac, guard duties will continue as scheduled. Darious, you must be here to help all of us get through the rest. Your brothers will emerge in ten years, and we will all need sustenance and help so plan accordingly. And Jarrod – bring me the other queens when they awake. It will be soon you have to find out when and bring them to me quickly."

Everyone paused to listen to her as she sent forth her orders. The guards went to work while Darious helped Colin and his newborn brothers into their coffins, sealing them in.

He took one last turn of the room to ensure everyone was where they were meant to be. When he leaned in to kiss his mother's forehead, she whispered to him, "The war has begun."